I'LL BE DAMN IF I DO, I'LL BE DAMN IF I DON'T

I'LL BE DAMN IF I DO, I'LL BE DAMN IF I DON'T

TALE OF COURAGE AND SURVIVAL

Shay Janai

To my readers:

Don't let your past determine your future. Everyone has a story, and every story is different. The people who hurt you are going on with their lives, while you're stuck on what happened to you in the past. I know it hurts; I know it sucks, and I know you have wounds we can't imagine you feel like you can't heal from. Put in the work on your mind and heart, and get the help you need. Show them they didn't break YOU!

Your crown may Tilt, but never let it fall off, King's & Queen's.

Shay Janai

ShayJanil

Shayna Janai

ShayJanai

Table of Contents

Prologue

"God won't give you no more
than you can handle."

This was one quote I hated hearing while growing up and all through adulthood. Why do I have to go through so much just to appreciate life? People always say, "Don't grow up too fast," then they turn right around and expose the same children to the exact things they asked them not to do. The law is supposed to protect children, but some people in positions will prefer to take money over doing what's right. I was confused, hurt, and fed up with God, the world, and just people in general by the time I was eighteen. I know this sounds crazy as hell, but you are just going to have to understand what I've been through. Don't get me wrong, I know everyone has a story, but for a long time my story was all I seen. I didn't have time to watch or wonder about anyone's life but my own. I put one foot in front of the other and did what I had to do to survive. The number of things I had seen at an early age was unbelievable, so let's just start at the beginning.

Chapter 1

Farida

I t's dark out here, and I'm scared walking down the road all by myself. I've never been anywhere alone, but what four-year-old has been? I was playing with my toys when I heard my brothers talking about killing our auntie in her sleep, but since I was still a child, I didn't understand what they were talking about. Our aunt took us in after our mom died in a car accident. That day, my brothers walked into my room and told me that my auntie had been hurting them, and that they needed to keep me safe before they killed her. My brothers, Amari Jr, Omari and Zane, were always nice to me, and so I did what they said. They picked me up and pushed me out the bedroom window, with Dalila in my arms. Then they told me to walk to the gas station we would always go to, stating that a man with a red truck would pick us up and keep us safe.

I was scared, as it was so dark and cold out there. I started crying before I even got close to the gas station. Once inside, the clerk noticed I was alone and then asked where I came from. I told the clerk that my brothers said a man was going to pick me up, and the clerk immediately called the police. I looked at the phone and asked if I could have it. I was only four years old, but my grandparents made sure that if I didn't learn anything else, I knew how to dial their number. Every time I came to visit, they would make me practice repeatedly on the phone pad until I got it. I grabbed the phone and dialed my grandparents' number, and they answered. I tried to explain, but at age four, my words are not noticeably clear. Then the clerk took the phone from me and told my grandparents where I was. Suddenly, the police and child protective services arrived and began questioning me as I was screaming, scared and overwhelmed. I later realized that the police got my address from speaking with my grandparents, and then they took me back home. My aunt was pissed when she opened the door and saw me. She was steaming with rage when she found out what my brothers did. Now, all these people in her business and y'all know black folks don't want anyone in their business or house. I didn't know much at an early age, but I knew we would definitely get our asses whooped after all these people had left. This goes with the saying, if one did it, everyone gets beaten just to make sure I got the right one.

Three weeks later, my aunt signed her rights over quicker than you can spell spaghetti for the boys. It's five of us: Zane, Amari Jr, Omari, Farida, and Dalila. We all have different dads besides Amari and Omari. Mom was raising us all, and just our luck, none of our daddies fought to get us after our moms' deaths. How do you manage to get three bad baby daddies? This is definitely some black folk's shit. Zane went with some of his father's family members. Amari went with his dad because he was his Jr., but he didn't take Omari. His exact words were "I'm not raising two kids by myself." That meant Omari was going to foster care. Foster care homes were full back then, so the kids went to juvenile, but we called it juvie. This left my little sister and me at home with my aunt.

Chapter 2

Omari

We were tired of getting beaten by our aunt. I don't think an aunt, let alone anyone, is supposed to be beating on you. Our mom never did this to any of us. Whenever we got into trouble, she would take things away from us but would never beat us. I'm thankful our aunt took us in after losing our mom, but she is beating our asses just because the sun is bright hell. I was at school, telling a friend what we were going through at home, when he said he had been telling his uncle everything that's been happening and that his uncle wanted to talk to me after school. His uncle, Mike, picked us up after school, and on the ride home, he told me he could take the girls and keep them safe, but not the boys. The he gave me a knife to kill my aunt. He told me it would be self-defense, and we talked over the plans for tonight. He told me that when the police showed up to tell them, my sister got scared, picked up my younger sister, and ran out of the house. When we went outside, we couldn't find them. I followed everything but the time frame. I didn't think that mattered because we just got our ass whooped again with an extension cord, butt naked, for not cleaning as well as she wanted. Hell, we thought we did an amazing job because Mom used to work with us and showed us how to clean things. This lady clearly beat us because she could and didn't need a reason. Beating all three of us drained her ass. When we found out that she wanted to take a nap after beating us, we thought it would be the perfect time to kill her. We decided to put Farida and Dalila out the window first because the loud front door would wake her up. My brothers and I were standing in our aunt's room by the door with the knife, trying to figure out who was going to stab her because we were all scared. We were whispering, but no one wanted to do it. Then Zane said, "I'll do it with y'all scary self." We looked at him like he was a damn fool because he was the oldest and should have done it anyway. Zane got the knife and tiptoed into the room by her bed, and the wood floors started creaking loudly. At this point, I just knew she was going to wake up and beat our asses again. Zane finally got by the bed and held the knife up, and his dumb ass turned around and asked us where to stab her. We rolled our eyes because we knew he had seen all the Law & Order shows we watched with Mama. Mama used to make us watch all her shows, including first 48. We whispered to stab her in the heart, Zane, so we get it right the first time.

When Zane turned around, our aunt's eyes opened like she felt a spirit watching her. We all ran to our rooms as she jumped up, realizing what we were doing. She started screaming at us to get naked so she could beat our asses next year. "Y'all want to be grown, I'm about to show y'all grown." How is it that black parents' lingo always comes with extra threats?

However, we got saved by the doorbell because I was sweating bullets. When we heard the doorbell, our asses let out a breath of fresh air. For the few minutes we were saved before this beating went down. Aunt Wendy opened the door to the police, and blue and red lights were flashing down the whole block. I looked down and saw Farida and Dalila and said, 'She is about to bury our bodies now for sure." Zane and Amari were speechless. They just sat there looking with their mouths wide open. The police and child protective services came in and told my auntie everything. Farida's young ass told everything that Smokie didn't tell Craig on Friday. Wendy's eyes turned towards us, and it was like we could see the rage coming off her body. The police officers started asking us questions about the guy, Mike, my sister had mentioned. I stepped up like I was on the stand and told the whole truth and nothing, but the truth so please help my God. I told them everything about Mike and that my auntie has been beating us since taking us in, and that's why we were trying to protect our sisters, and we were going to kill our aunt. Everyone's eyes in the room turned to Wendy, and the officer asked if this was true. Now, why do officers ask criminals questions they know they are about to lie about? No, you have got to do your job. You think a criminal is about to help you lock them up. Of course, she denied it, and now a case was open for further investigation. We had to remove our shirts to show if we had any physical wounds. What we didn't expect was for Wendy to know so many people. That case got dropped as quickly as ice melts in water. Wendy signed her rights over for us boys, but kept the girls, so she would keep getting a nice check from them.

Amari Jr.

Before the case with child protective services was over, Wendy whooped all our ass all the way to the courthouse to sign her rights over. Thank God my daddy decided to step up and take me, since I'm his Jr. My brother Omari was crying when our father said he couldn't take us both. I felt for my brother because he drew the short stick. I promised him we would stay in touch and protect our sister, Farida, because the way Zane would look at her wasn't normal. We had to fight him a few times for trying to touch her like he wasn't her brother. It looks like we had to protect them from a distance, but at least he was outside the house and away from the girls. I was just happy to be starting over and getting to know who my dad is and getting away from our crazy ass aunt, Wendy. I hope I never have to see her again.

Omari

No one wanted me, so I ended up in the system. Life isn't fair! This is some bullshit. Everyone wants to keep their kids innocent and avoid telling them as much as they can about the world, as if they know they will be here to explain things. It's better to hear from your parents about race and life difficulties you will face than to let a child figure it out alone without knowing all the pieces. But here I was finding out the world, and that the system doesn't give a shit about an older black boy. I got locked up in juvie like I was a criminal because they had nowhere else to place me. I don't know my future, but this feels and sounds like they are putting me in a position to fail. How did I go from cleaning up our mother's home, excited to wake up on the weekends because I knew our mom had an amazing day and great food planned for us, to live in juvie, and I had never committed a crime?

My aunt only hit the boys, so I'm praying that it's a God listening who protects my sisters, and maybe she wouldn't hurt them. Amari and I promised to stay in touch as much as they allowed us to protect the girls. In some unspoken words, we knew we weren't going to be able to do anything since we physically weren't there, but maybe that's what Mom called faith when she spoke about God. Dalila was an infant, so we knew our aunt wouldn't hurt her or do anything bad to her.

Chapter 3

Farida
(Years Later)

After Wendy signed her rights over to the courts for the boys, she still needed a babysitter, and Zane volunteered. He was my brother so initially I felt safe because he's the oldest and at least I get to see one of my siblings. But that changed as I got older. I couldn't stand to be around Zane! My stomach would turn, and I would feel like I wanted to throw up instantly. I had a lot of dreams every night about him. It's like my mind blanked events or hiding them deep inside, but my dreams at night will bring them back. I would wake up screaming in pain and sweating. When I finally told Wendy about these dreams, she would just let me know that they were just dreams and that the events never happened. But to me, everything about them felt as real as my hands. I finally settled back down, and I dozed off, saying, "My dreams are not real." I was staring at this red clock on the wall, watching it jump to the next second, and my brother stood in front of me with his dick out, saying, "Just keep licking it like a sucker and I'll give you some candy, or I'll tell Wendy you've been bad so she can beat you again." I just did what he told me and kept staring at the red clock on the wall as he grabbed my head to guide me. Suddenly, I noticed the window was open, and I jumped up and jumped out the window while trying to avoid a huge ditch that was behind the apartment. I began running, and when I looked back, I saw that the red door of the apartment had flung open, as my brother chased me down. When he caught me, I screamed in pain and blacked out. I woke up to pain between my legs and him looking at me right in my face. He said he tried to take it easy on me, but since I wanted to run, he had to teach me a lesson. I tried to fight him off me, but there was nothing I did that stopped him or the pain I felt between my legs. Zane reached for the lamp and smashed it on my face, and I blacked out again. When I woke up, my eyes were blurry, but the pain between my legs was more like pressure now. I finally got a clear view, and Zane has invited his friends over, and one is on top of me, and I had no more fight left in me. When they noticed I was awake, they said, "Let's have more fun now that she is tired of fighting." Now they took turns and put me in various positions, and now the boys face my front and back, and the pain came back as they force themselves into every hole I have.

I woke up sweating and screaming, wondering what was wrong with me. Did Zane touch me at such an early age that my brain couldn't process it, and hid it deep down? I was overwhelmed with different thoughts. Then Wendy approached the room, asking what was wrong and I told her that my dreams were real and that I could feel them. Wendy looked at me and said she was tired, and

I kept waking her up screaming so Zane will never watch my sister or I again, but black folks don't report anything about family members. "You're okay, your still here, he didn't kill you and your woman parts needs to be broken in so you can eventually make some money, go to bed!" I looked at Wendy like she was the dumbest person in the world. Zane hadn't watched my sister or me in years and I made sure of that by doing it myself so what the hell is Wendy talking about! Then who the hell she thinks she is telling me my woman parts need to be broken in, so I can sell some pussy for money! I know damn well she is not thinking about pimping me out.

Chapter 4

Omari

I just busted this teen's head wide open for playing with my new cellmate. I'm older now, so no one bullies me or people around me. Wendy did enough damage to traumatize me for life. Being locked up with criminals and some other boys who fell in the system like me, you have to learn a thing or two about taking care of and protecting yourself. It's been years since I've been locked away and thrown away like some trash that people forgot about. I haven't seen my siblings in years and wondered what they are doing and how they are doing. I've been studying the guard's routine, and tonight is the night I'm breaking out of here. This one guard got a thing for fucking little boys, and when he leaves his station tonight, I'm getting out. I'm on the cleaning crew tonight, so it's perfect timing. Just like clockwork at 9:00 pm, he heads to what we call the newbie bed, and he left his keys like a dumb ass on the desk as he has done in the past because he is thinking about the wrong thing. I grabbed the keys to remember which key goes to which door, and just like butter, I slide out until I feel the breeze of air hit my face. I ran like I've never run before. I hid for the next few days behind houses and dumpsters. Homelessness at 16 isn't what I thought my life would be like. In juvie, I learned a lot about stealing and how to feed myself with what I have. I stole from grocery stores and convenience stores that didn't have security on site. I also stumbled across where Aunt Wendy moved and watched their routine from a distance. I planned to catch Farida and Dalila walking to the bus stop tomorrow and surprise them.

Chapter 5

Farida

Wendy had gotten her boyfriend now. I didn't like him or the way he looked at me. I try to never get caught with him because it's that unspoken feeling. When she leaves, he always leaves too. I'm 14 now, so I know when something feels off. I just must try not to piss Wendy off about her man because I don't want to get beaten again until she decides she doesn't want him, as she did with many men in the past. Wendy comes into my room and tells me to wake up because she is going to work early. That means I must get my younger sister dressed, then myself, cook breakfast, and head to the bus stop. Dalila's bus normally comes first, and if mine did, I would miss the bus. Put Dalila on the bus and walk to school. I feel like I'm already a parent, and parenting comes with a few things you learn to make your life easier. I learned to get myself dressed first before my sister because kids are hard to wake up and they move slowly. To knock some wrinkles out of our clothes, I head to the dryer that is outside in the garage and throw our shirts in there since we don't have an iron. I head back inside to put some toast in the oven for our breakfast sandwiches and go to my room to finish getting dressed. Normally, I get dressed and cook at the same time, so when I wake Dalila up, everything is done, and we can eat our sandwiches on the way to the bus stop. I'm in my room putting my pants on, and I feel like someone is standing behind me, and as soon as I can turn around, Mike, my aunt's boyfriend, is choking me. He started pulling my pants back down and pushing me on my bed. I was kicking and trying to scream, but he gripped my throat tighter and told me to shut up. He released my throat and covered my mouth with his hand. I started screaming and hitting him as he pushed me face-first into the pillow. I heard his zipper slide down and closed my eyes because I knew all too well about what was about to happen. I heard a pop sound and turned my face to the side as Mike's grip loosened and wiped my eyes to clear the blur from crying, and I saw my brother Omari with a gun in his hand at my room door.

Chapter 6

Omari

I can't believe this nigga was about to rape my sister. I watched my sister go to the garage where the washer and dryer were to throw her school shirts in there. I said to myself that my sister is one of those girls that don't believe in ironing. She went to the back door, and I noticed it was the kitchen, and she was making some food, and a brother was hungry. She left the back door open rushing, and I noticed my aunt's car was gone early today so it's perfect timing to teach her about locking doors behind herself no matter how soon she is coming back out to get her school shirts. I peeped around and didn't see a car for who I assumed was Wendy's boyfriend and from the looks of it he always leaves when she does. I overslept today so I didn't get a chance to get here real early. Just like a big brother wants to scare their sister but teach a lesson at the same time. We are two years apart, but she can learn how to protect herself when I'm not around. The moment I go through the back door I see my sister has made eggs and sausages and put toast in the oven and got some strawberry jam on the counter. I was proud my little sister learned how to cook because I'm hungry as hell. I hear loud noises and sounds like my sister is struggling so I get my gun out I picked up off the street and head towards the sounds. I get to Farida room and see this grown nigga unzipping his pants as my sister fights. I popped the safety off and shot right at his head, and he fell right next to Farida twin size bed on the floor. Farida was crying and when she noticed me, she ran right to me and hugged me. I held my sister in disbelief about what was about to happen to her if I wasn't there. One thing about being around criminals, you learn a lot.

I told Farida she had to be strong and not say a word. She had to stick to her school schedule today because I had to hide his body. Farida ran to Wendy's room, got Mike's keys, handed them to me, and said his truck is parked a few houses down because he is married. I told Farida to go get dressed, and I helped with Dalila, who slept through everything in her room. They got their breakfast and ran to the bus stop while I pulled Mike's truck around the back of the house before it got light outside. I wrapped his body up in trash bags. The good thing about the early 80's there was no cameras on the traffic lights yet, so you just had to avoid driving by stores with cameras outside. I started stealing a lot this way to feed myself.

I used to steal cars, so I know this chop shop and illegal spot where they burn evidence. I pulled up to the hood burn spot location like Denzel Washington in Equalizer and tossed Mike's body in the pile they were already burning while everyone focused on grabbing the next evidence pile that indeed could lead them to life in prison today. I spoke to a few homies and had some simple conversations. I picked up so much weight in juvie, I looked like a wrestler at 16 years old, and nobody was fucking with me. I went from never doing anything criminal to turning into the criminal the system created by putting me with criminals. The only difference I said if I'm going to do this life, there's no getting caught! A nigga had to be on his game. Mistakes get you caught or dead.

I drove to the chop shop next. You can tell Mike loved his truck because he put so much work in it, from hemmed pipes, new rims, and new red seats. The shop busted that bad boy down fast. Since I used to steal, I always had gloves before food. No prints, no case. I was walking back to my aunt's house when a homie pulled up on me and gave me a ride to the store, then to my aunt's house. I immediately went to cleaning because I knew my aunt went to the pool hall right after work, so she would not be back until 9:00 pm that night, and that was perfect timing for me. The goal was to get rid of this nigga body and vehicle before all the neighborhood old ladies saints wake up and call the police officers for a random African American boy walking around, they've never seen before. I started with the kitchen because I didn't want my fingerprints anywhere in this lady's house. One thing about my mama, she knew how to clean and showed us. Her law & order shows always played in my head on what not to do to get caught. I wiped down the back door and headed to bleach my sister's room down. I moped and bleached down her room four separate times. No blacklight was about to detect shit when it came to my sister. When I shot Mike, he fell on the floor and a blood spitter hit my sister, her comfortable seat, the wall and of course the floor where her body fell. That was an easy cleanup for me because the bullet didn't exist. After I finished, I looked over my handy work, pleased with the outcome. Now it was time to dispose of the mop bucket and all my trash. I need to burn all evidence. I told my homie to come back and pick me up and pull behind the home I had some to dump at the spot to burn and his ass was right on time. The only way to get a Black person to show up on time is to offer money and he knew he was about to get some paper. Afterwards, he dropped me off at my sister's bus stop and I hid behind some buildings as I waited for her bus and Dalila bus to pull up.

Chapter 7

Farida

I did exactly what my brother said. I was thankful this man didn't put his hands on me and rape me. So, the last thing I was going to do was say anything. My sister's bus arrived, and my bus right after. On the bus ride to the school, I said I blanked out stuff from when I was younger, so this will be no different. Forget and move on. I went to school and acted just like myself, doing the same predictable routine. I'm not going to lie, my heart was skipping beats thinking about what would have happened if Omari didn't pop up, but I had to get those thoughts out of my head fast. I participated in class to make sure I was seen as always, because school was always my haven. I had friends and teachers who loved me, and it was a regular day for me. I couldn't wait until I saw my brother. I got off my bus and Dalila bus pulled right up after me, and I spoke to the bus driver as I waited for them to bring my sister. I wanted to keep my same routine.

Omari

I was watching the girls get off the bus. I was ducked off in some bushes, waiting for the other kids to go down the road before I walked back with the girls. When they were alone, I popped up because it was a spot where no houses were, so it was perfect to talk. Our little sister was so young she didn't know who I was. I whispered in Farida's ear that I'll be outside in the garage at her normal time to talk and give updates. I told her if the police show up, don't say anything because they have no evidence, no body, no vehicle, and no statements, so don't say shit. I told her I loved her and would always protect her, and I meant that shit!

Chapter 8

Farida

When I got in the house, candles and incense were lit to hide the smell of bleach. The house was cleaner than my aunt ever cleaned it. My room was spotless. I had a new bedroom set that was a close color to my old set, almost identical. Now that I see everything, I feel so much better. My auntie got home and asked me why I cleaned up so much, and I told her I was bored. Just my luck, she told me I need to get bored more often! Just lying through my teeth but smiling because her boyfriend was gone. About two hours passed, and she asked if Derrick had said anything this morning before leaving, and I told her I hadn't seen Derrick this morning when I was leaving. Auntie said that's weird because his phone and everything were gone. A quick thought popped up in her head, and she said, "I know this nigga hasn't left me and went back to his wife, low down ass."

Chapter 9

Omari

I chilled out behind the dumpster not far from KFC. I used the money from selling the truck to the chop shop to buy some food. I'll lie low tonight until I get to see Farida in the morning. The next day came fast because I couldn't sleep that well with all this going on. I headed towards my aunt's house and hid behind some bushes until I knew she was leaving. When she left for work, I saw Farida go to the garage to put their clothes in the dryer, and I snuck in there. As soon as we saw each other, she ran over and gave me a big hug, and I assured her everything would be fine. I told her she must stick to her schedule and not tell anyone what happened. I explained it will be a few weeks before they link Auntie to having a relationship with Derrick. They would have to go through phone records and clear his wife first. When they pop up, act like you don't know anything, and I gave her a few questions they may ask, and stick to those answers I gave you. I told Farida I love them both and I was going to go without seeing them the next month so they don't connect us to anything and told her to keep her predictable schedule just in case I need to reach back out or if things don't, pan out I have an exit plan but know I'm somewhere around watching, keeping both of you safe. In the meantime, I'll find Amari Jr.

Chapter 10

Farida

I hugged my brother and thanked him so much as tears fell down my face. I understood and will stand behind my brother and follow everything he said. I went into the house and got ready for school. I didn't tell Omari about my dreams about what Zane did to me or that my aunt beat me. I was sure he would have more bodies on him, and I didn't want him to give up the possibility of having a life. I wanted to see us make it out of this. Why does life place such heavy burdens on children? The law is meant to protect us, yet it fails, and when we protect ourselves, suddenly it becomes a crime that brings punishment! I'll hold this secret until death.

A few weeks passed, and my aunt took her anger out on me. I swept the floor as instructed, but it wasn't as good as she wanted, so a beer bottle struck my head. I'm so used to getting hit, I don't even pass out anymore. I just take the hit and use it as encouragement to keep going because it must be a better life out here that I don't know about yet.

Chapter 11

Farida

Two months later, as I walked through the door from school two police detectives was talking with my aunt in the living room. I started walking to my room like they always say, "Stay out of grown folks' business." I took my sister to my room and turned on Tom & Jerry. I put my ear to the wall to listen because my aunt's walls were so thin that I heard every time she had sex. The police told her his wife reported him missing, but they were having problems because Derrick was sleeping with multiple women. I can tell by my aunts' response she was shocked she wasn't the only other woman. I'm in the room laughing because why would you think you're the only woman when this man clearly has a wife and doesn't stay here every night. My aunt told them the last time she seen him and assumed he went back to his wife since he hasn't been responding to her many calls and texts. The detectives told them they would check her alibi to verify she worked her shift and if she hears from him, let them know. That was the first and last time we ever seen the detectives and my aunt never bought Derrick name up again.

Chapter 12

Omari

I have been laying low, but I am getting money now. That homeless shit wasn't for me. I have got to make some money so I can take care of my sisters. I found my knuckle head brother Amari Jr and my dad. To be honest my brother doesn't look better off like I thought he would be. He is getting food and clothes, but they are raising him to be a thug. His head messed up, he thinks he about that life but he not. I tried to talk to him, but he wouldn't listen. I'm going to try to save my siblings, but I'm not working on a miracle if they ass don't listen. I haven't really fucked with the oldest brother because his mind has been messed up since he was a child. He been needing a therapist at an early age, but you know black people run from therapist like they pulling a gun on you. He used to brag about a lot of sexual things he did to Farida when I was younger and couldn't defend myself. But now, if I ever catch him, I'm going to kill him. Farida was so young, so I doubt she remembered anything, and she hasn't said anything so I'm not going to put that on her unless she ever asked me. One less situation to have on her mind.

Chapter 13

I have been in the drug game since I left Farida and Dalila. I have been working these corners and stacking bread and getting my rank up. I'm about to be 18 in two days so I won't have to hide out anymore. I got so many young dudes under me working, I'm keeping my hands clean. I have been watching my sisters grow up from a distance. Farida smart as hell and got all types of awards for her grades, different science events and some high school public speaking events. A hard life will do that to you; make you push harder in what you're good at to try to get out of the current situation you're in. I'm happy as hell she pushes to learning instead of what life gave her. Farida plays sports too and I have been purchasing all her gear and giving the money to her coach, letting her know I got her. On birthdays I would leave money, cards, flowers in her school locker for both of them because girls like that shit for whatever reason. I haven't had a father to raise me but I know my sister need to know it's some good men out her so I'm gone buy everything they need so they don't need another man to do it or give up anything to get it. It's crazy how we are just two years apart, but our birthday is the same day. When I turn 18, she will be big 16 and I see she has been studying for her driving test. I'm going to surprise her with a cash car to have more freedom. Something we never had!

Chapter 14

B ig 18 in the building! I'm finally free from the state. This shit feels like I have been in prison all my life and now I am getting freedom. Money stacked and I already had a ride. Now it's time to get legal with everything. I'm about to go buy another car and gift it to my sister for all her hard work. Farida take her driver's test today and I know she going to past the test today with her smart ass. I headed to check out some rides and I didn't see anything that was good enough to put my sisters in because safety first. I went to the Honda dealership next and found the perfect car for my sisters. I figured I might as well work on our credit now. I might be street smart but in juvie they had a lot of books, and I liked to read a lot, and I learned a lot about life and God in those books that help and helping me become the man I need to be. I'm just out her here surviving the hands I was dealt with. I called Farida finally and she was so happy on the phone and told me she passed her driver's test in her friend's mom's car. I was happy and congratulated my sister for another accomplishment. She is making my parents and I so proud because I look at how our lives are and look at how she is turning it around writing another story for her life and I'm trying to be here for it all. I asked her to speak with her friend's mom and I told her that I had a surprise for Farida, and could she meet me at the dealership after they go pick up Farida new license. I already had some fake work check stubs and Farida already had a legal job with check stubs and I wanted us to both sign for this car so we could work on both our credits. She worked at McDonalds, was good at sports, stayed out of trouble and got good grades, she deserved this and much more. Farida was so happy when she seen me, she ran up and hugged me so tightly I thought she was breaking me. We knocked out the paperwork and I put the minimum amount down. I told her I had the note covered every month but she needed to pay for the insurance every month so she can establish paying bills. I know Farida was mature beyond her age, but big brother just had to make sure. I educated her to drive when needed because she is a new driver on the road, to always buckle both of them up since she is basically a mom to our little sister. It's like I'm the dad to my sister's and Farida the mom to our youngest. We just both trying to make something good from all this bullshit we have been through. We just got to make it out!

Chapter 15

F arida handed me a book before she left. She has been saving her money and paying for a GED class for my birthday, and she already highlighted the book for me to study and had notes attached. The first note warmed my heart the most because no one has ever loved me the way my sister has. The small memories of our mom, fade as I get older.

Letter from your little/Big sister:

I know you are wondering why I'm giving you this but it's self-explanatory. I made it this far because you gave me every opportunity to succeed and chase my dreams. Now it's time for me to have your back! I can't make it out by myself; you must make it out of the game too.

Don't think I don't know where you have been getting this money from. The game gone lead you to jail or the grave. We need to jump ship, move and leave this state and start a new life. I have our sister, and I need you to get this legal education and apply what you learned on the street and multiply it legally. When I'm 18 I'll be applying for guardianship over our sister, and we will need somewhere to live and that's where you come in. I'm getting good grades and I'm going to college and I'm going to let these sports pay for it and while I'm knocking that down I need you working a legit job and keeping our sister head straight. I'm going to go Pro and take care of us. I got you a fast-paced GED class, you will be done in six months. Then I will help you apply for college so think about who you want to become or what you would like to major in. You will be busy for the next three years. Go to school during the day and handle your business at night. I got our sister! I've been protecting her, and auntie haven't put her hands on me or her in a long time because I been threating to get her check cut off, I found she has been receiving money on us. She haven't touched us since. I learned a lot about law with research, and I found some papers while I was cleaning Auntie room from mom lawyers. I attached the letters behind this letter. Mom had a check set up to go to her sister's account if anything was to happen to her and cut her a small check for caring for us, hence why she decided to take us in. Mom must not have trusted her sister that well because she set all the kids up to (receive a large lump sum) when we turned 18 years old instead of giving everything to her sister. We received $40,000.00 each. So go get your money and be ready to research the school that offers me a scholarship in two years so we can get out of here. I'm over this and I want to live and see that world, it has got to be more out there we haven't seen. If you need help studying for the GED class or your college work, call me or text me. I love you always superman.

Chapter 16

Farida

My 16th birthday was the best day. I got to see my brother, skipped school and I got a nice car for Dalila and me. I knew Omari had been around like a ghost but it was different when I finally saw him. My aunt is about to flip out about this car but it's in my name and Omari and she will not touch it. One thing my brother did was make a name in the drug game because even my aunt scared of him now. She will not touch this car or try to take it. I'm headed to go pick Dalila up from school and making sure I buckle her up just in case his crazy ass watching us like a stalker. After I picked up Dalila, we headed to the store to get some snacks and something for me to cook dinner and we went straight home as instructed. I'm sure my brother will ride pass to make sure I'm not out joy riding. I wish I was outside when he does it too so I can be like, where do I have to go in this small town? What he needs to be doing is getting ready for that GED class that starts tomorrow.

Chapter 17

The next two years flew by, and graduation was approaching. I was ready and happy to move on to the next part of my life. I made a lot of school friends but none that I'm attached to, and no boys were on my mind. I was already 18 and my aunt should be getting served papers within these next few days from the court. I applied for guardianship for my sister, and my brother already had a nice spot, legal job and an associate degree in business. With what we had and my scholarship to Miami, FL to play basketball, we were good and solid in the court case. My brother hired a lawyer, and I gave them everything I had on my auntie and all the pictures through the years of abuse. I decided to skip prom, and I didn't want to waste the money, nor did I care about one night. My mind was only focusing on school and getting out of here. By the time I got home my aunt was served and pissed when I walked through the door. She came up to me like she was about to swing on me, and I stood straight up and starred her down because I promise I'm not the little girl you used to beat on anymore!

Aunt Wendy

This bitch done served me and think she about to take my check. This bitch 18 and can go but I got a check coming the next few years for the little brat sister of hers. I been nothing but good to those little bitches. Taking them in after my stingy sister died and this the thanks I get. I should have let her brother keep raping her. Then my ex-boyfriend Derrick was supposed to pay me $2,000.00 to fuck her and he disappeared on me, and I still never seen him again. Farida is nothing but a whore using some dude to buy her a car and give her some money. I got a job, and I'm going to win and put her out on the street as soon as the court is over. I got something for her ass. "Farida, what the fuck is this? You are serving me now? I got something for you."

Farida

If she didn't put her hands on me, I was fine taking verbal abuse. I was already used to it. Bitch, hoe, no good slut, Hefer, you name it, and I've been called it. Sometimes I feel like verbal is worse than physical abuse. I never understood why she did all of this, and we never did anything to her. But the last day she hit me was it. She locked my sister outside in her panties and bra with no shoes, threw some food out on the porch, and told her to eat like a dog. Everyone in the house was taking a nap when Dalila woke up hungry. Dalila tried to make some noodles in the microwave and forgot to put water in the bowl and smoked up the whole house, I woke up to my aunt yelling, "Eat like the dog you are since you are so hungry!"

As I approached the kitchen, I seen my sister crying through the screen door and what she had on and how she was talking to her, and I flipped out and picked up a chair and beat my auntie ass. She did me as she please but my sister I draw the fucking line. That was the last time she ever crossed that line with my sister again.

Chapter 18

Court time came right after graduation, and I'll have to leave for Miami soon for summer training and summer school. My aunt walked into the court dressed like a first lady at church. I don't go to church often, but I knew she was about to put on a whole Jerry Springer show here. The court got started, and my lawyers were ready. My aunt saw my lawyer and was very confused, and I'm sitting here thinking, yeah, you thought I was doing this by myself? Judge of course let her go first and she told him all this good stuff about how she fed us, clothed us and took all the kids in after her sweet sister passed aways. It was a situation where the boys tried to sell their sisters, and she had to sign her rights over to protect us. She was all smiles and sad faces when needed. It was like some bad acting in a Tubi movie.

My lawyer asked to approach the bench because he had documentation about everything my aunt had just stated. The judge looked over all the documents, my lawyer came back to his seat and stated, "Judge Mrs. Wendy did take her sister's kids in after her death, but it was for the money, not because she cared for them." My aunt stood up screaming lies as if this isn't a court room and not a reality show. The judge told her to be quiet, just like they were quiet when you presented your statement, so sit down!

My lawyer continued. "Judge, we are simply asking you to look at the evidence and grant Farida care for her sister, as she has been her whole life. Farida has a job at McDonalds and her paychecks as well as her bank accounts and receipts over the years are all attached to what I gave you. Farida had bought the food to cook and feed them both. She gets her dressed in the morning for school and drops her off and picks her up. I also attached statements from the neighbors, bus drivers, and teacher that Farida even at 14 years of age was always dressing her sister, feeding her and handling her transportation. If her bus came before her sister's she would miss the bus, wait on her, put her on, and then walk to school. At 16 years of age, her brother brought Farida a car. They both saved money to make life easier to care for their sister. Farida's job at McDonalds paid for the car insurance and her brother got a job at a law firm to pay for the car note. Their aunt never knew they were in touch, but they helped take care of each other. Mrs. Wendy never got Farida's report cards, attended any school events, or any of Farida's basketball games. Farida has many scholarships to go to many schools, and she recently accepted a scholarship to Miami State University where she has a full ride and housing. Your honor, you might be wondering how Farida will care for her sister and focus on school and sports at the same time. Their brother Omari is one of the children Wendy gave up. Omari was in foster care, but despite how his childhood went, he got his GED 6 months after turning 18. He immediately went to college after and holds an associate degree in paralegal studies and now works for a law firm where he makes $60,000.00 a year. I included everything in the documents. When the children turn 18 years of age their mom had set up a policy for each child to receive $40,000.00, Farida and Omari collected the money off the policy, and both invested in some real estate in Miami. I saved this for last because it breaks my heart to say this, and it will break yours too. I'm just happy that out of all the bad things that happened in their life, something good is finally happening to them, and they need this one more thing to make this complete. The system failed them, so let's get it right this time. Judge I have pictures of Farida with beating marks, voice recording and video footage from Farida personal phone as new as a few weeks ago. I think you should watch these first because Mrs. Wendy admitted to doing a lot of things while she was home alone. Mrs. Wendys also took rent each month from Farida even though she received a check each month for her clothes, food and any other needs as left by her parent's instructions. Since Farida was paying for her room rent, she put up a camera outside her room door in a wall picture, and it caught Mrs. Wendy's physical and verbal abuse of Farida on many occasions. The video footage had dated stamps. On the very last recording, when Mrs. Wendy got served. She admitted that she was getting paid to let her boyfriend rape Farida, and she in fact knew her oldest brother was molesting Farida and never reported it. Farida and Omari are set financially, mentally and emotionally to provide a loving and safe home for their sister Dalila. If you grant Farida guardianship they will be ready to fly out in two days to start their new life as the University already knows Farida situation and what she is trying to do. Housing is provided by the University."

Farida

My aunt's face looked like someone had slapped her, and she couldn't believe it. The fact that she thought I was coming to court without anything was beyond crazy. I knew she wouldn't notice the camera or anything else. She wanted to make me pay for a room every month, and I figured a video camera wouldn't hurt. I also have many videos and pictures on my phone. As soon as I could start taking pictures, I did. When we were younger and she won custody with just our word against her word, I wanted to make sure this never happened again.

The judge needed time to review all the footage, pictures, and all the documents my lawyer gave them. He called for a recess. Two hours later, the court was back in session. You can tell by the judge's face that he was sad, mad, and in disbelief at what he had just seen.

Judge

"I honestly don't know where to start. I looked at all the evidence in disbelief that a family member could act this cruelly. I went deeper into the case because how did your aunt get custody in the first place. Then I see those statements when you went to the gas station and your brother's statements about why they did it. Then your aunt's best friend was your case worker and that's how it got dropped so fast. The law, the people, and your aunt failed all of you after the loss of your mother. Your mom's neighbor actually fought to get custody of all of you, but being your aunt was family; the courts always grant family custody. I'm looking at what you and your brother overcame as a proud parent myself. I'm proud of you, Farida, and I'm proud of your brother, Omari. You are granted custody of your sister, Daila Louise Whiteside. But don't celebrate just yet! You've also done our job for us and got evidence against your aunt that we can use to press charges.

Wendy, I hope you realize that you didn't break Farida. You wanted the children to be nothing, and they are becoming exactly what you will never be. You had more than enough money left from their mom to have you set for life and them but instead you decided to be evil. On top of whatever jail time you receive, as the court will be picking up this case, you will be paying all the money you received back when you get out of jail. You will never be able to live without thinking of them. I feel disgusted by your behavior as an aunt and embarrassed that you got to scam the system for many years. Take her into custody and read her rights!"

Congrats Farida and I wish you nothing but success along your journey and keep fighting to be heard. You did it! You made it! Go make a great life together.

Chapter 19

Omari

I flipped all my money into this legal hustle. Farida was right, it's like weight has been lifted off my shoulders and I don't have to look over my back anymore. My crew knew what was up when I was in the game, and it wasn't a problem passing my throne down. I'm not clearing as much money the legal way as I did in the game, but it's clean and we're still set. We won't have to worry about anything. I found a lawyer's office that was hiring in Miami and I'm all set to go. We just had to get this court shit over with. After Farida finishes school, I'm going to get my bachelor's degree and go to law school. I know I can't change everyone's future, but I will try to make sure what happens to us doesn't happen to another child. For now, I will work and keep up with our investments and invest more because Farida, sports and education are top priorities while I learn to care for our little sister.

I was sitting in the back of the court watching everything go down, and Farida smart ass played chess, checkers, and whatever smart-ass games. I would hate to go to court fighting her. The lawyer was worth all his money, and we're going to keep him around just in case. I felt another weight get released off my shoulders when the judge congratulated Farida. I got up and walked out of the court to wait for them outside. It's something about getting what you know you deserve, and it is finally happening that brings you a sense of peace. While I'm thinking about my future life and this trip we are about to take, my phone rings. My homeboy Troy is calling, "What's up, little lawyer?" I just laughed and told him, "You still can't take the hood out of me; you might need me one day." After a few laughs catching up, Troy said he had some bad news and was trying to see if I was in a spot to talk. I told him, yes. Troy said my brother Amari Jr. got shot fucking around with some dude's wife, and he died. Troy wanted to know if I wanted the husband to get handled. I told Troy let the husband live, my brother head was fucked up bad, but we gone get the body and bury him right but let me get back with you because my sister walking over and I have to tell her this news.

Chapter 20

I f it isn't one thing, it's another. My little sister ran right into my arms, telling me I'm her dad now since she's going pro and taking care of us. We all just laughed. I told our sister to get in the car and let us talk for a minute. Farida looked me dead in the face and said," Shit, what's happened now?" I told her Amari Jr. got shot, and he didn't make it.

Farida

It's like paying a car note off and your car breaks down right after. Any little piece of happiness gets snatched right away. This is what we are going to do because their daddy didn't have life insurance for Amari. We gone go get settled in Miami and come back and bury him. He only had us so no big service and we gone slide right back out. His $40,000.00 automatically split between the rest of us so we gone send him off right. I know this is a sad moment, but we are going to make it through this like we did everything else. We have to start going to church to start making sense of this life of ours. From what I got from reading the bible is it's full of short stories and it's not one person something didn't happen to, so in this life it's not saying everything was going to be easy but the storms we go through will determine who we will be. Omari, "So you're basically saying Eve should have never bitten the apple?"

First off, I truly believe Man bit the apple and that's why men have the Adams apple and lie so much. Secondly, no way Eve should of bit that apple because men hardheaded as hell. I basically had to force you to go to school. I see the vision of what our life could be like and God seen the vision without anyone else. You need steps along the way to finally see the vision I see for us. It's okay because that's why women are smarter than man. Omari just laughed and said, "Get in the car silly girl, its hot." We went back to my aunt's house and packed up a few items. We had two days to spare, and we decided to drive to Texas and get a small vacation before Life hit us again.

If you enjoyed this book and want to know what happened to their other brothers, the funeral and life after leaving.

Follow along with my other future books.

Dialog

To my amazing Whiteside Family, I want to thank you all for forcing education, reading, showing compassion and creating a space for me to learn about God in the most powerful loving way. God didn't give me no more than I could handle and I could testify to that every day. Every storm that came my way God never gave up on me even when I gave up on myself. I love you and I'm thankful for Grandma and Pawpaw legacy they left.